I dedicate this book to my wife,
without whose love and patience
it would not have been. R. J.

First published in Great Britain, Canada,
Australia and New Zealand in 1991 by North-South Books,
an imprint of Nord-Süd Verlag AG, Gossau Zürich, Switzerland.

British Library Cataloguing in Publication Data

Johnson, Russell
The princess and the carpenter.
I. Title
823.914 [J]

ISBN 1-55858-104-9

1   3   5   7   9   10   8   6   4   2
Printed in Belgium

THE PRINCESS AND THE CARPENTER

By Russell Johnson

Illustrated by
Bernadette Watts

North~South Books
New York

There was once a king who had a beautiful daughter called Rosie. The King longed for Rosie to marry the very best husband heaven could provide.

In the spring, when the birds and flowers began to stir, he asked his daughter: "Will you marry Prince Ferdinand? He has a fine kingdom of farms, orchards, and pretty streams."

"Not for the finest kingdom in the world would I marry him," she answered, proudly tossing her long golden hair. "For the only prince I will ever marry must have a smile in his eyes."

In the summer, when the hot sun shone all day long in the bright blue sky, the King asked his daughter: "Will you marry Prince Walter? He has a beautiful kingdom, with meadows, cornfields and winding rivers."

Rosie replied: "Not for the most beautiful kingdom in the world would I marry him, for the only prince I can ever marry must have a smile in his eyes."

And her own eyes brimmed with tears as she pulled her hair awkwardly behind her ears.

In the autumn, when the wind tore the red and yellow leaves from the trees, the King said to his daughter: "Will you marry Prince Maximillian? His kingdom is wonderful, with great forests, rolling hills and deep lakes."

Rosie shook her head sorrowfully, saying: "Not for the most wonderful kingdom in the world would I marry him, for he has no smile in his eyes."

The Princess gazed out the window of her room, as the chill wind blew away the gold from her hair and the roses from her cheeks.

In the winter, snow and ice covered the whole kingdom, so it seemed only death lived there. The King spoke again to his daughter: "Will you marry Prince Peter? He has a magnificent kingdom with moors and craggy mountains."

"No, I will not," Rosie sighed. "I can only marry a prince with a smile in his eyes."

Again she gazed out of the window. But this time she noticed a lonely tower standing on a mountaintop.

"Father," she said, "I will go and live in that lonely tower, and if I look far and wide every day, maybe I will find a prince with a smile in his eyes."

And so she left her father's home.

After some time the King visited his daughter and was very upset by what he found. The wind and rain whistled through the broken roof and windows of the tower. The floors and doors were damaged, and the rooms were empty and forlorn.

At once, the King decided his daughter's dreadful dwelling should be repaired and he ordered his servant to fetch Sebastian, the best carpenter in the whole land.

Roderick found Sebastian in a forest clearing, kindling a fire. Roderick told him the King's wishes.

"I cannot come to the King right away," said Sebastian. "I have caught a fish and must cook it now. Come back another day!"

The next day the servant found Sebastian in the forest and begged him to come to the King.

"No," replied Sebastian firmly, "I have snared a rabbit and must cook it right away. Come back another day!"

The third time the servant found Sebastian, he was sitting on a tree-stump sharpening his tools. "I am now ready to visit the King," he said. "And I will carry out all his wishes." So he packed his tools into a green handcart and, whistling merrily, trundled off to the King to get his instructions.

When he reached the tower, he carefully repaired the roof so there was not even one tiny hole left. The sun was so hot Sebastian took off his coat and tossed it to the ground below.

"That's a good idea!" said the Princess and she took off her embroidered cloak and tossed it out of the window.

Next Sebastian cleaned all the chimneys. He was covered with soot from head to foot, so he jumped into the stream and splashed about till he was clean.

"That's a good idea!" the Princess laughed, kicking off her silken shoes, and she splashed in the stream too.

Then Sebastian refitted all the floorboards so not even the tiniest draught came through. But the room looked drab, so he painted the floor blue to match the sky.

"That's a good idea!" said the Princess, and she took a brush and painted flowers all over the walls.

Finally, the hard-working carpenter set about repairing the locks on the big entrance door. It was such a beautiful day. The sun shone warmly, the birds sang merrily, flowers blossomed everywhere.

"Oh blow it all!" shouted Sebastian. "Let's go fishing!"

"That's a good idea!" laughed the Princess.

They went to the river and caught a fish. Sebastian built a fire and Rosie hung the fish up to cook.

Sebastian wove a crown of fresh flowers and offered it to her. It was then that she saw the smile in his eyes.

The King was delighted with Sebastian's work and overjoyed to see his daughter's happiness. "Have you met a prince with a smile in his eyes?" he asked.

"Oh yes, dear father! And here he is!"

The King turned to Sebastian. "If you marry my daughter I will give you riches beyond your wildest dreams and when I die you will be king."

But Sebastian replied: "I have no need for riches. Look, my pockets are empty! And I have no desire to be a king. I'm perfectly happy as a carpenter."

"Then you cannot marry my daughter," said Rosie's father. "Her husband *must* be the King."

"Well," said Sebastian. "I have finished all the work here, so now I will be going."

Sebastian told Rosie he was going home. Taking her hand he said, "I love you very much. Please, will you marry me?"

"I don't know," she said. "Can a princess marry a carpenter?"

"You know the answer in your heart," he replied.

When Sebastian left, taking his tools with him, it seemed to Rosie that he took away her sunshine too.

"I'm sorry Rosie," said her father sadly. "You will just have to be queen all by yourself."

"No!" she declared. "I don't care about being queen, I love Sebastian. I love him and I will marry him!"

She hitched up her skirt, picked up the crown of flowers Sebastian had made, and set off along the road. The King smiled to himself as he watched his daughter disappear into the distance.

Rosie walked many days and eventually came to Sebastian's home. The front garden was full of vegetables and flowers, chickens and geese pecked the grass. The door of the house stood open, although she did not see anyone.

When she stepped inside, she knew in her heart she had found her true home.

The house was very snug, with carved chairs, shelves of books, and cooking pans hanging on the wall. A kitten and a puppy played together.

Rosie was extremely hungry. So she caught a fish in the nearby stream, as Sebastian had taught her, and took herbs and vegetables from the garden. Then she lit the fire and began to cook.

"Well, that's a good idea!" someone shouted from the doorway. Turning round, she saw Sebastian, her carpenter.

"I will marry you," she said happily.

He came to her and kissed her and with a smile in his eyes, he said, "That's the best idea of all."